The Littles

Have a Happy Valentine's Day

To the memory of
Winnie Moffitt and Hugh Malone,
who were married on Valentine's Day, 1888
—JP

Adapted from *The Littles Have a Wedding* by John Peterson.
Copyright © 1971 by John Peterson.

ISBN 0-439-42499-2

12 11 10 9 8 7 6 5 4 3 2 1   3 4 5 6 7 8/0

Printed in the U.S.A.
First Scholastic printing, January 2003

Adapted by **Teddy Slater**
from THE LITTLES HAVE A WEDDING
by **John Peterson**
Illustrated by **Jacqueline Rogers**

SCHOLASTIC INC.
New York Toronto London Auckland Sydney
Mexico City New Delhi Hong Kong Buenos Aires

One cold, breezy day,

a tiny glider landed

on the roof of Mr. and

Mrs. Bigg's house.

Cousin Dinky Little

and Della Kett got

out of the plane.

They went into the house

through a secret door.

The other Littles
were waiting in
their apartment
inside the Biggs' walls.

They were all so tiny,
the Biggs never knew
they were there.

Cousin Dinky had big news

for his family.

"Della and I are getting

married," he said.

"On Valentine's Day!"

"Vera Long and Sam Tower
are getting married
then, too," Della said.
"So our wedding can be
in the Longs' house."

"I wish we could all
go," Mrs. Little said.
"But the Longs live
a whole block away.
Granny and I could
never walk that far."

"Don't you worry,"

Cousin Dinky said.

"I have a plan.

The whole family will be

going to this wedding!"

"I want to be the flower
girl," said Lucy Little.
"And I want to be the
ring bearer," said Tom.

Granny Little sewed a
fancy dress for Lucy.
It came almost to the tip
of her tail.
(All the tiny people
had nice long tails.)

Tom made a golden
wedding ring for Della.
It was just the right size.

Cousin Dinky told Tom
and Mr. Little his plan.
Then they sneaked into
the Biggs' rooms and
found a few things they needed.

The Littles were careful

to stay out of sight.

Only the cat, Hildy, saw them.

She was their friend.

On Valentine's Day,
Cousin Dinky led
the family outside.
"Ta-da!" he said.

"By golly!" said Uncle Pete.

"It's a balloon!

What are we waiting for?"

Cousin Dinky helped Granny

and Mrs. Little into the basket.

The other Littles tied the

strings around their waists.

"Ready to lift off!" cried Cousin Dinky.

Slowly, the basket
began to rise.

The Littles went across

the Biggs' yard and

down the garden path.

The strings kept the balloon

from flying off into the clouds.

But suddenly, a puff of
wind lifted the balloon
higher . . .
and higher.

"Help!" cried Tom.

"Help! Help!" cried Lucy.

"Hang on!" Cousin Dinky
shouted. "I'll save us."

Cousin Dinky climbed
up to the balloon and
let out some air.
Whoosh!
The basket floated
down to earth . . .

. . . and landed right outside

the Long house.

The Littles ran inside.

There was no time to lose.

Della and Cousin Dinky had

to be married at the same

time as Vera and Sam.

Cousin Dinky led the way
to a secret room behind
the Longs' living room.
Everyone changed into
their wedding clothes.

Cousin Dinky and Della

stepped through a tiny door

in the back of a large clock.

The clock was on

the fireplace mantel shelf

in the Longs' living room.

From inside the clock,

the Littles could see

and hear the big people.

But the big people had

no idea the Littles

were there.

"I now pronounce you
husband and wife,"
the minister told
Sam and Vera.
Little did he know
he was also marrying
Cousin Dinky and Della.

"Hooray for

the bride and groom!"

said Tom.

"And happy Valentine's Day

to everyone!" said Lucy.